FLOWER FAIRIES

THE MEANING

of FLOWERS

PLANTAIN AND MOON-DAISY DANCING TOGETHER,
ALL THROUGH THE BEAUTIFUL SUNSHINY WEATHER.

Poems and pictures by
CICELY MARY BARKER
◆
FREDERICK WARNE

An Introduction

Flowers and trees have possessed symbolic meaning since classical times, but the idea that flowers could form a language was first introduced into England by Lady Mary Wortley Montague, during a visit to Turkey in 1716. She wrote in a letter to England, "You may quarrel, reproach, or send letters of passion, friendship, or civility, or even news without inking your fingers."

When Cicely Mary Barker came to create her beautiful Flower Fairies books, she imbued both the poems and illustrations with a sense of the flower's traditional meaning. Flowers have long been associated with fairies, and her little books, instantly popular since 1923, appealed to the public interest in flowers, fairylore and superstition.

This book explores the meanings, fairy uses, remedies and magic spells of flowers and plants, beautifully illustrated by Cicely Mary Barker's exquisite watercolours and extracts from her poems.

AGRIMONY

THANKFULNESS ◆ GRATITUDE

The Agrimony may have earned this meaning because of the likeness of its flowers to the little hand-bells once carried by hermits when collecting alms for the poor. In many places, it is actually called Gratitude.

Snake Bite Cure

For an effective antidote to snake bite, infuse the flower in water and drink.

Magical Abilities

Agrimony forms part of a potion that enables the carrier to recognise witches, and by itself, the flower is said to have the power to draw forth thorns and splinters from the skin.

ALDER

Because it grows near water, the Alder is protected by water spirits. It is said to understand human speech, and will weep if it hears it is to be felled.

For a Feversome Patient

Place Alder leaves in the patient's nightclothes so that they touch the skin. In the morning, the fever will be lowered.

ALMOND

STUPIDITY ◆ INDISCRETION
THOUGHTLESSNESS

ALMOND BLOSSOM

◆ HOPE ◆

Career Advice

To ensure business success climb an Almond tree.

APPLE

◆ TEMPTATION ◆

The Apple became the emblem of temptation when Eve first succumbed to its sumptuous promise in the Garden of Eden.

Fairy Gifts

When harvesting the apples, always leave a few on the tree for the fairies to ensure future good harvests.

Apple Blossom

Apple Blossom is the symbol of preference because unlike other sweet-scented flowers, its dying blossoms are followed with fruit.

You'll fly away! But if we wait with patience,
Some day we'll find
Here, in your place, full-grown and ripe, the
Apples you left behind –
A goodly gift indeed, from blossom-babies
To human-kind!

Ash

◆ GRANDEUR ◆

Ash Man

According to Norse mythology, the gods created Askr, the first man, from an Ash tree. Druids made their wands from Ash twigs, and witches chose Ash from which to fashion their witchdolls. Its closeness to humans meant that it was used as a predictor of human life and well-being: if a parent wanted to find out if their weak child would ever grow strong, they would split an Ash tree and pass the child through it. The Ash tree was then bound up again, and if it grew soundly, then it was a sure sign that the child would grow strong again too.

Safe Spot

Stand in the shadow of an Ash tree to avoid venomous snakes and mischievous fairy spirits.

To Relieve Earache

Heat one end of an Ash stick in the fire until the sap bubbles from the stick. Place the warm sap in the affected ear to relieve the pain.

Bee Orchis

INDUSTRY ◆ ERROR

This rare flower gives the impression, at first sight, that a bee is in the flower, busily collecting pollen. Hence its first meaning, 'industry'. But on closer inspection, one realizes that the bee is actually a part of the flower itself, and that your eyes mistook you – hence its second meaning, 'error'.

There's a sight most rare
that your eyes may see:
A beautiful orchis that looks like a bee!
A velvety bee, with a proud little elf,
Who looks like the wonderful
orchis himself...

Beech Tree

◆ PROSPERITY ◆

Place for Prayer

Say a prayer beneath a Beech tree and it will go straight to heaven.

Black Bryony

◆ BE MY SUPPORT ◆

Freckle Remover

Black Bryony is a lucky plant, and was used to remove freckles.

To Increase Wealth

Fashion a human figure from a Bryony root. Place a pile of money beside the figure and wait for your wealth to increase.

Blackberry

LOWLINESS ◆ ENVY ◆ REMORSE

I'll tear your dress, and cling and tease,
And scratch your hands and arms and knees.

The bramble is the symbol for envy because of its habit of choking nearby plants just as they put forth their new shoots.
Its fruit is the symbol for lowliness because it grows wild and is free for all to pick.

Blackberry Law

The bramble is sometimes called by another name, Lawyer, because of its prickly branches, which so swiftly trip or entangle passers-by.

Thorny Remedy

Crawl through a bramble bush backwards to cure rheumatism, boils, rickets, whooping-cough and eczema.

BLACKTHORN

◆ CONSTANCY ◆

Blackthorn is the emblem of difficulty because its thorns are notoriously difficult to untangle from the clothes on which they cling.

Blackthorn Winter

The cold days of March are sometimes called 'Blackthorn Winter'.

To Release Captive Children

Thorn trees are places where fairies love to dwell. To release children held captive by the fairies, make a fire of thorns on the peak of a fairy hill. Your children will be returned to you.

BLUEBELL

◆ CONSTANCY ◆

The Scottish name for this flower (apart from harebell) is Deadmen's Bells for it is said that to hear the ring of a Bluebell is to hear one's own death knell. For this reason, it should never be picked.

Warning Bells

Be wary of walking through a Bluebell wood for it is a place of concentrated fairy magic and enchantment.

Box Tree

◆ STOICISM ◆

The Box Tree is a slow-growing evergreen plant, unaffected by the changing of the seasons. Its enduring qualities have made it ideal for the practice of topiary, and it has become the symbol of stoicism.

Have you seen the Box unclipped,
Never shaped and never snipped?
Often it's a garden hedge,
Just a narrow little edge;
Or in funny shapes it's cut,
And it's very pretty; but –
But, unclipped, it is a tree
Growing as it likes to be.

Burdock

IMPORTUNITY ◆ TOUCH ME NOT

The Burdock is the symbol for importunity because of the tenacious ability of its seeds to cling to animals or clothes. The plant also carries the meaning 'touch me not', warning unwitting passers-by against becoming inextricably tangled with its burrs.

Burdock Root Tea
━✳━
Burdock roots when boiled and strained provide a pain-relieving drink for mothers in labour.

Buttercup

CHEERFULNESS ◆ INGRATITUDE
CHILDISHNESS

Despite its association with cheerfulness and childhood, this little yellow flower is some-times called Insane Herb from the belief that its scent is enough to drive a person mad!

Buttery Chin
━✳━
Hold a Buttercup beneath your chin. If it casts a yellow shadow, you are fond of butter.

'Tis I whom children love the best;
My wealth is all for them;
For them is set each glossy cup
Upon each sturdy stem.

CANDYTUFT

◆ INDIFFERENCE ◆

This evergreen shrub is the symbol for
indifference because it is unaffected by the
changing of the seasons – it bears its flowers
come rain, snow or frost.

Why am I 'Candytuft'?
That I don't know!
Maybe the fairies
First called me so…

CHERRY TREE

DECEPTION ◆ GOOD EDUCATION

The wild Cherry tree is the symbol for
deception because although it blooms as
beautifully as the cultivated cherry tree, its
fruits are inferior. The cultivated Cherry tree
is the emblem of good education because
careful pruning produces a better fruit when
the blossom is over.

Poison Protection

Carry a sprig of Cherry tree in your pocket
and poison ivy will be unable to harm you.

Wish Upon a Cherry

If two people wish while sharing a cherry,
their wishes will come true.

Cherry Tea

Cherry tea is a flavoursome drink and is an
excellent tonic to restore health after a
long illness.

CHICORY

◆ FRUGALITY ◆

Chicory has this meaning because it was used to eke out coffee during rationing years.

Chicory Magic

Chicory has many magic powers. Explorers of new lands hung it on their banners to make themselves invisible, gold prospectors put Chicory root in their pocket to bring them luck, and the plant is said to be able to open any lock.

COLUMBINE

◆ FOLLY ◆

Columbine is associated with folly because its flowers are so like the cap and bells of the traditional court jester.

CORNFLOWER

◆ DELICACY ◆

An old English name for the Cornflower is Hurtsickle because medieval sickles had difficulty cutting through their wiry stems.

Cure for Short-sightedness

Cornflowers are renowned for their amazing ability to heal short-sightedness. They make up a medicine called eye-water which was said to be so successful that spectacles would never be needed again.

COWSLIP

EARLY JOYS ◆ WINNING GRACE
PENSIVENESS

The Cowslip earned the meaning of 'early joys' because these pretty yellow flowers mark the return of Spring.

Keys to Heaven

In some places, the Cowslip is known as 'keys to heaven'. The legend goes that when St. Peter heard that wicked souls were trying to enter heaven through the back gate, he dropped his keys in horror. They fell to earth, and where they landed, a bunch of Cowslips sprung up, their blossoms resembling keys.

Fairy Uses

Cowslips are an invaluable fairy flower – their blossoms provide shelter from the rain and unlock the way to fairy treasure.

Human Uses

Effective in restoring memory and youthful bloom and beauty, but it is most commonly used in the flavouring of Cowslip wine.

Headache Tea

Put a whole Cowslip in hot but not boiling water. Brew for five minutes. Strain and drink.

CROCUS

ABUSE NOT ◆ YOUTHFUL GLADNESS

Crocus Sleeping Pills

The Crocus can be distilled to make a powerful sedative, but over-consumption may result in the total collapse of the patient. The importance of moderation when using this flower-medicine earned it the meaning of 'abuse not'.

Crocus Caution

Crocuses have the ability to inspire love, but be wary of collecting them – they are said to drain strength.

Daffodil

◆ REGARD ◆

Daffodils should be treated with utmost care and should never be picked. They will bring good fortune to the person who carefully avoids treading on them whilst walking.

Daisy ◆ Double Daisy

INNOCENCE ◆ PARTICIPATION

The Daisy derives its English name from 'day's eye', being one of the first flowers to open its petals in the morning.

The Double Daisy became the symbol of participation in the time of knightly tournaments. If a lady allowed a knight to wear a Double Daisy on his shield, it meant that she accepted and requited his love. But if she wore Double Daisies in her wreath, it meant that she was still considering it.

Cure for Insanity

Steep the Daisy in wine and drink a small dose every day for fifteen days.

Recipe for a Romantic Dream

Ingredients: One pair of shoes; a pillow; a handful of Daisy roots.

Method: Hang your shoes out of the window. Place the Daisy roots under your pillow. Sleep, and dream of your lover.

A Little Spell

Simmer a quantity of daisy roots until well reduced. Drink the potion to grow small.

REMEMBER!
Never transplant wild Daisies to a cultivated garden – it is unlucky!

Dandelion

◆ LOVE'S ORACLE ◆

Dandelion came to mean 'love's oracle'
because of the ritual of blowing on its
seed-head – 'She loves me, she loves me not',
the last seed revealing the true answer.

Dandelion Tea

Infuse the roots of a Dandelion in hot water,
strain and drink. The tea is an excellent tonic
and promotes a feeling of well-being.

Fortune Teller

If the seeds blow in your face, expect an
important letter.

Dog-violet

◆ FAITHFULNESS ◆

Violets are unlucky flowers, except in
dreams where they signal a change for
the better.

Dogwood

◆ DURABILITY ◆

I was a warrior
When, long ago
Arrows of Dogwood
Flew from the bow.

Dogwood is the symbol of durability
because it is one of the hardest woods. It
used to be called Dagger-wood because
it was used to make spears,
javelins and arrows.

Elder

Dangers of Elder Wood

There are virtually no safe uses of Elder wood. A garland of Elder hung on the front door will attract demons, and burning Elder logs will bring the devil into the house. Furniture should never be made of Elder wood, least of all cradles. The Elder fairies will pinch the child that lies in it black and blue, before pulling it out by its heels. Witches lurk beneath the branches, and Elders have the sinister habit of uprooting themselves after dark to stare through the windows of houses.

Virtues of Elder

Elder does have a few positive uses. During daylight hours, it protects fairies against witches and evil spirits. Pregnant women may safely kiss the Elder to ensure good health and fortune for the coming baby and an Elder tree is a good place to take shelter in a storm – it will never be struck by lightning because it is said to be the tree from which Christ's cross was made.

Before Taking a Branch

If you are determined to use Elder wood despite its dangers, always ask the tree's permission before taking a branch – witches are fond of transforming themselves into elder trees and it is never a good idea to offend a sorceress.

Elder Bark Tea

Brewed elder bark makes an excellent medicine for mothers after child-birth, to sooth pain and replenish energy.

Elderberry

Elderberry Magic

Gather the berries on St. John's Eve to acquire magical powers and protect against witch's spells.

Fir Tree

◆ ELEVATION ◆

The Fir Tree is the symbol of elevation because of the great heights it is capable of reaching in its growth.

To Heal the Sick

Lay a branch from a Fir Tree on the sick bed to aid the patient's recovery and ensure future health.

Forget-Me-Not

TRUE LOVE ◆ REMEMBRANCE

The origin of this flower's name is based on an Austrian folk-tale. Two lovers were walking the bank of the Danube. The girl saw a pretty blue flower floating on the river and expressed her sadness that it would be swept away. Her lover leapt into the water to retrieve the flower, but was overcome by the waves and began to drown. He threw the flower to her saying with his last breath, 'Forget me not!'

Keys to Treasure

Like the Cowslip, the Forget-me-not has the power to open the way to fairy treasure.

Press the flower against the mountainside where the treasure is concealed and watch the secret cavern walls fly open.

Foxglove

◆ INSINCERITY ◆

The Foxglove derives its name from 'little folk's-gloves' because the fairies wear its flowers as hats or gloves. But some people believe that the flower earned its name because sly foxes used the florets as gloves to muffle their tread when out stealing chickens. Whatever the reason, avoid this fairy flower – its other names are Goblin's Gloves, Witches' Thimbles and even Dead Man's Fingers.

Geranium

COMFORTING ✦ STUPIDITY ✦ FOLLY

The stunning colour of the Geranium is a comfort and a joy to look upon, but its bitter scent is disappointing and reveals its beauty to be mere folly.

Gorse

✦ ENDURING ✦

'When Gorse is out of blossom,'
(Its prickles bare of gold)
'Then kissing's out of fashion,'
Said country folk of old.

O dreary would the world be,
With everyone grown cold –
Forlorn as prickly bushes
Without their fairy gold!
But this will never happen:
At every time of year
You'll find one bit of blossom –
A kiss from someone dear!

The Gorse bush is the symbol of endurance because it always has a few yellow flowers in bloom come rain or sun, all throughout the year. Thus, people came to rely on its show of blossoms and could confidently say, 'When Gorse is out of blossom, then kissing's out of fashion'

Guelder Rose

WINTER ✦ AGE

Remedy for Nerves

Guelder Rose bark tea has a most soothing effect on the nerves, and can be used effectively in the control of cramps, asthma and hysteria.

Harebell

SUBMISSION ♦ GRIEF

When dim and dewy twilight falls,
Then comes the time
When harebells chime
For fairy feasts and fairy balls.

They tinkle while the fairies play,
With dance and song,
The whole night long,
Till daybreak wakens, cold and grey,
And elfin music fades away.

The Harebell is also known as Devil's Bells.
It is a dangerous flower to pick because it is
commonly used by witches.

Harebells for Honesty

Harebells inspire truthfulness – he who wears
one will find it impossible to lie.

Hawthorn

♦ HOPE ♦

My buds, they cluster small and green;
The sunshine gaineth heat;
Soon shall the hawthorn tree be clothed
As with a snowy sheet.

O magic sight, the hedge is white,
My scent is very sweet;
And lo, where I am come indeed,
The Spring and Summer meet.

The Hawthorn (or May) symbolises hope
because its blossoms are a sign of spring. Its
blossom-laden branches were gathered on
May Day and used to decorate the house in a
symbolic gesture of bringing Spring and hope
into the home.

Like all thorn trees, the Hawthorn is a sacred
meeting place for fairies. The Bretons named
it Fairy Thorn because they believed it to be
haunted by fairies.

HAZEL

RECONCILIATION ◆ PEACE

The Hazel offers protection from danger – a cap of Hazel leaves and twigs ensures good luck and safety at sea, while a sprig of Hazel will protect against lightning. Water-diviners use Hazel wands to detect water.

Nuts of Wisdom

According to ancient lore, the little Hazelnut is a receptacle of knowledge, wisdom and fertility.

Wedding Prophecy

If you can break a Hazelnut in three pieces at a single stroke, take it as a sign that you will be married soon.

HEART'S EASE

◆ THOUGHTS ◆

An old name for the Heart's Ease or wild pansy is Jump-up-and-kiss-me. The finder of the first wild pansy of the year will be blessed with eternal joy and remembrance.

HEATHER

◆ SOLITUDE ◆

I come, I come! With footsteps sure
I run to clothe the waiting moor;
From heath to heath I leap and stride
To fling my beauty far and wide.

A Fairy Feast

Heather thrives in wide open windy moors and so became the symbol of solitude. Fairies, who also enjoy living undisturbed, are said to feast on stalks of Heather.

HELIOTROPE

DEVOTION ◆ FAITHFULNESS

Well-beloved, I know, am I –
Heliotrope, or Cherry Pie!

Heliotrope is the Greek word for 'head turned towards the sun', so named because its flowers follow the sun throughout the day, making this famously sweet-scented flower the symbol of devotion and faithfulness.

To Reveal Cheating Spouses
❋

A bunch of flowering Heliotrope placed in a church will reveal those who have not been true to their marriage vows – they will be rooted to their seat.

HOLLY

ENDURING LIFE ◆ FORESIGHT

The leaves of the Holly are prickly up to a height of around ten feet, but above this, where there is little need of protection, the leaves are smooth at the edges. Its berries sustain birds when other foods are scarce, and so for these two reasons, the Holly bush shows its foresight.

In Case of a Storm
❋

A piece of Holly in the pocket will protect against lightning.

To Win Favour with Fairies
❋

Decorating the house at Yuletide with branches of Holly and berries delights the fairies and so brings good fortune.

HORSE CHESTNUT

◆ LUXURY ◆

My conkers, they are shiny things,
And things of mighty joy,
And they are like the wealth of kings
To every little boy…

The Horse Chestnut, though a fine tree, has few practical uses – its wood is not fit for timber and its conkers, though much loved by children, are not edible. It is a purely ornamental tree and therefore became the symbol for luxury.

An Old Chestnut
❋

Horse Chestnuts are vessels of good fortune and in Japan, dried chestnuts are emblems of success, victory and conquest.

IRIS

Iris is named after the goddess of the rainbow because of its many hued blooms.

Freckle Remedy

Blend together a handful of Irises with a small measure of honey. Spread evenly upon the freckles, leave for a few hours and remove. If freckles have not completely disappeared, re-apply.

Uses of Iris

Iris root powder, or Orris root, has a strong odour of violets and enriches the scents of other substances. It therefore came to be used to scent violet perfumes and to bring out the bouquet of wine.

KINGCUP

Golden king of marsh and swamp,
Reigning in your springtime pomp,
Hear the little elves you've found
Trespassing on royal ground –

'Please your Kingship, we were told
Of your shining cups of gold;
So we came here, just to see –
Not to rob your majesty!'

LARCH

AUDACITY ◆ BOLDNESS

Sing a song of Larch trees
Loved by fairy-folk;
Dark stands the pinewood,
Bare stands the oak.
But the larch is dressed and trimmed
Fit for fairy-folk!

The Larch became the emblem of audacity and boldness because it roots itself in the windiest hill tops and the poorest soils.

LAVENDER

◆ DISTRUST ◆

It is said that the asp and viper like to lurk beneath the Lavender, so it is wise to approach the plant with caution and distrust.

Advice for a Bride

Bring a sprig of Lavender into the house for protection against marital cruelty.

Warning Fire

Lavender is burned on St. John's Eve to keep witches away.

LILAC

◆ HUMILITY ◆

A five-petalled Lilac is a lucky find, but should not be given to a friend in hospital lest it cause a relapse in health.

LILY-OF-THE-VALLEY

RETURN OF HAPPINESS ◆ CHASTITY

Lilies-of-the-Valley, flowering in May, bring tidings of warmer weather and hence symbolise the return of happiness. They have long been emblems of humility and chastity because of their pure white blooms and bowed heads.

MALLOW

◆ MILDNESS ◆

See, my seeds are fairy cheeses,
Freshest, finest fairy cheeses!
These are what an elf will munch
For his supper or his lunch.
And I never find it matters
That I'm nicknamed Rags-and-Tatters,
For they buy my fairy cheeses,
Freshest, finest, fairy cheeses!

Mallow Sweets

The whole Mallow plant, including its
nutritious root, was once used to make syrups
and sweets. Nowadays, it is more commonly
used to flavour herbal teas.

MARIGOLD

◆ GRIEF ◆

It is because I love you so,
I turn to watch you as you go;
Without your light, no joy could be.
Look down, great Sun, and shine on me!

The Marigold, opening at sunrise, closing at
sunset, and following the sun all day, is an
emblem of the sun and a reliable floral clock.

Marigold Uses

Marigolds have many practical uses – they
can be used as a herb to flavour stocks and
soups, or as a dye to colour the hair yellow.
This bright flower, with its glorious sun-like
colours, also has the power to strengthen and
comfort the heart, and was appropriately used
to cure melancholy and the plague.

Marigold Jam

A little Marigold jam taken at breakfast will
protect the consumer from
witches and enable her to
see the fairies.

Michaelmas Daisy

◆ AFTERTHOUGHT ◆

The Michaelmas Daisy does not show its bright flowers until the autumn, when most other flowers are already passing over, and so it became the emblem of afterthought.

Mountain Ash

◆ PRUDENCE ◆

They thought me, once, a magic tree
Of wondrous lucky charm,
And at the door they planted me
To keep the house from harm.

Witch-Wood

Mountain Ash or Rowan has great powers of protection. Since ancient times it has been used to charm away bad spirits and used to be known as Witchentree or Witch-wood.

Rowan Magic

Butter churns were made from rowan in order to keep the fairies from meddling with the butter and casting spells upon it, while a rowan whip could keep a bewitched horse under control. The Druids used rowan wood to conjure up spirits who were then forced to answer their questions.

Mulberry

◆ I SHALL NOT SURVIVE YOU (BLACK) ◆
WISDOM (WHITE)

The black Mulberry tree earned this meaning because it is such a slow growing tree that it was said that the person who planted it would not live to taste its fruit. This is probably just as well since the devil himself uses the berries to black his boots, and it is therefore considered most unlucky to eat them.

Narcissus

◆ EGOTISM ◆

A Greek legend tells of a beautiful shepherd who fell in love with his own reflection in a pond, and drowned when he tried to reach it. His body was turned into the Narcissus that we know today, which became the symbol of self-love and egotism.

Bride's Curse

There is only one occasion on which these beautiful spring flowers are inappropriate – they should never be present at a wedding lest they bring unhappy vanity upon the bride.

Nasturtium

◆ PATRIOTISM ◆

When Nasturtiums were first introduced into Europe from their native America, they were grown in the kitchen garden and enjoyed as a food. The stalks were boiled and served as a vegetable, while the leaves, flowers and seeds were eaten in salad. An old recipe requires the seeds to be 'bruis'd with a polished cannon-bullet' before being tossed into the salad.

Pickled Pods

Nasturtiums were widely grown in the seventeenth century when it was believed that the pickled seed pods would prevent scurvy in sailors at sea.

NIGHTSHADE

◆ TRUTH ◆

Hide you your hands behind you
when we meet,
Turn you away your eyes.
My flowers you shall not pick, nor berries eat,
For in them poison lies.

Nightshade Remedies

Nightshade is also called Fevertwig, because it once formed part of a popular remedy against fever. In very small doses, the Nightshade even provided an effective antidote to opium poisoning.

Nightshade Eyedrops

The other name for Nightshade is Belladonna because Italian ladies used it to dilate their eyes and make them shine. This beauty tip was known to Queen Elizabeth I, who used the eyedrops daily.

Sinister Uses

Nightshade forms a vital part of a witch's flying ointment, and though it is the emblem of truth, the drinker of Nightshade juice will believe whatever is told him.

NIGHTSHADE BERRY

'You see my berries, how they gleam and
glow,
Clear ruby-red, and green and orange-yellow;
Do they not tempt you, fairies, dangling so?'
The fairies shake their heads and answer 'No!
You are a crafty fellow!'

'What, won't you try them? There is naught
to pay!
Why should you think my berries poisoned
things?
You fairies may look scared and fly away –
The children will believe me when I say
My fruit is fruit for kings!'
But all good fairies cry in anxious haste,
'O children, do not taste!'

Oak

◆ HOSPITALITY ◆

The Oak has long been considered a potent tree, imbued with the powers of peace and protection. It was worshipped by Druids and Norsemen, but it was the Celts who made it the symbol of hospitality, their most respected virtue.

The Marriage Dance

In Pagan times, marriages were often celebrated under oaks – the bride and groom danced beneath its branches for luck.

An Acorn Pendant

An Acorn hung around a child's neck will protect it from harm.

Old Man's Beard

MENTAL BEAUTY ◆ ARTIFICE

Old man's beard or Wild Clematis became the emblem of artifice because beggars used its stinging juices to cause ugly sores on their skin and so evoke greater pity and generosity from passers-by.

Periwinkle

◆ PLEASURES OF MEMORY ◆

Periwinkle Feast

Periwinkles have the power to inspire love: if
a married couple share a feast of Periwinkle
leaves, their love for each other will
be rekindled.

Pinks

BOLDNESS ◆ TEARS

You might learn a secret,
among the garden borders,
Something never guessed at,
that no one knows or thinks:
Snip, snip, snip go busy fairy scissors,
Pinking out the edges
of the petals of the Pinks!

Pink Drinks

In the Middle Ages, Pinks were used to
flavour beer, ale and wine, and later became
part of a medicine to cure melancholy – it was
thought that a drink made from their brilliant
blooms was sure to cheer the heart.

Pinks Vinegar

Ingredients: A handful of Pinks;
white wine vinegar, warmed
Method: Strip the flowerheads from the
stalks, and put into a glass jar until half full.
Pour over the vinegar to the top of the jar.
Leave to steep for two weeks in a
sunny place.
This recipe was one of the many 'cures'
for the plague.

Plane Tree

In ancient Athens there was a long avenue of Plane Trees that became a popular meeting-place for greek philosophers. They used to pace the long avenue amidst heated philosophical discussions, and so they appointed the Plane Tree the emblem of genius.

A Plane Remedy

To heal general ills, simply chew the bark straight off the Plane Tree. For a cold remedy, the bark should be boiled first.

Poplar

◆ COURAGE ◆

Hercules wore poplar leaves on his head when he descended into the underworld. The leaves were blackened by the flames of Hades. Everafter, the Poplar has grown black leaves and is the emblem of the courage of Hercules.

Poplar Bark Remedies

A piece of Poplar bark placed in the hair will cure a fever.

Poppy

TRANSIENT PLEASURE ◆ CONSOLATION

Opium, the drug made from poppies, has been used in some form for hundreds of years to bring relief from pain. A side-effect of the drug was that it induced a state of ecstacy that eventually wore off, and so the Poppy became the emblem of transient pleasure and consolation.

Dragon-lore

According to old English legend, the brilliant red Poppy sprung up out of the blood of a slayed dragon.

Cautionary Tips

Never look into the black eye of a Poppy for you will be struck blind, nor should you hold the flower too close to the ear for you may be struck deaf.
Be aware that should you pluck a Poppy, heavy thunder will result.

Poppy Uses

The Poppy can be used to drive away unwanted lovers. It can also bring luck if sniffed three times a day.

PRIMROSE

◆ EARLY YOUTH ◆

Primrose Spells

The common Primrose is a vital ingredient in numerous old spells and remedies.

It may be eaten with salt and vinegar to cheer the spirits, mixed with lard and made into an anti-wrinkle cream and blusher, distilled into a juice to restore speech to a dumb man, and left on the doorstep on May Day eve to keep witches away.

To See the Fairies

Primroses have the power to reveal the invisible. Consume them to see the fairies. Touch a fairy rock with a posy made up of the correct number of Primroses, and the way to fairyland will be open to you. But beware, for if the number of Primroses is wrong, you will meet your doom.

PRIVET

◆ PROHIBITION ◆

Here in the wayside hedge I stand,
And look across the open land;
Rejoicing thus, unclipped and free,
I think how you must envy me,
O garden Privet, prim and neat,
With tidy gravel at your feet!

Privet is the symbol for prohibition because it is cultivated as a hedge to keep out prying eyes.

RAGWORT

◆ EARLY YOUTH ◆

The Ragwort is the fairies favoured means of
travel. They utter the magic words, and the
ragworts uproot themselves from the earth
and turn into fairy steeds.

RUSH GRASS

◆ DOCILITY ◆

Rushes, with their strong but supple leaves,
have been woven into a variety of useful
objects, and so have earned the meaning
of docility.

RED CLOVER

◆ INDUSTRY ◆

O, what a great big bee
Has come to visit me!
He's come to find my honey.
O, what a great big bee!

There is nearly always a bee hovering around
the sweet-scented Red Clover. Its association
with these busy insects makes it the symbol
for industry.

ROSE

LOVE ◆ BEAUTY

Best and dearest flower that grows,
Perfect both to see and smell;
Words can never, never tell
Half the beauty of a Rose.

Scarlet Pimpernel

CHANGE ◆ LOVER'S SECRET MEETING

By the furrowed fields I lie,
Calling to the passers-by:
'If the weather you would tell,
Look at Scarlet Pimpernel.'

When the day is warm and fine,
I unfold these flowers of mine;
Ah, but you must look for rain
When I shut them up again!

Weather-glasses on the walls
Hang in wealthy people's halls:
Though I lie where cart-wheels pass
I'm the Poor Man's Weather Glass!

Self Heal

When little elves have cut themselves,
Or mouse has hurt her tail,
Or Froggie's arm has come to harm,
This herb will never fail.
The Fairies skill can cure each ill
And soothe the sorest pain;
She'll bathe, and bind, and soon they'll find
That they are well again.

(This plant was a famous herb of healing in
old days, as you can tell by the names it was
given – Self-Heal, All-Heal and others.)

Shepherd's Purse

◆ I OFFER YOU MY ALL ◆

Though I'm poor to human eyes
Really I am rich and wise.
Every tiny flower I shed
Leaves a heart-shaped purse instead.

In each purse is wealth indeed –
Every coin a living seed.
Sow the seeds upon the earth –
Living plants shall spring to birth.

Shirley Poppy

◆ FANTASTIC EXTRAVAGANCE ◆

A clergyman, who was also a clever gardener,
made these many-coloured poppies out of the
wild ones, and named them after the village
where he was the Vicar.

SLOE

◆ DIFFICULTY ◆

For a Healthy Heart

Sloe berries are unpleasantly sharp until they
have been mellowed by frost. Nevertheless,
eat the first three Sloe berries you see to avoid
getting heartburn that year.

SNAPDRAGON

◆ PRESUMPTION ◆

Snapdragon Charm

Conceal the Snapdragon secretly on your
person to appear gracious and fascinating. It
will also protect you from deceit and curses.

SILVER BIRCH

MEEKNESS ◆ GRACEFULNESS

Birch Spirit

Garlands of Silver Birch by the front door
keep demons away, but the spirit of the tree
can inflict madness and death.

Snowdrop

The Snowdrop, said to resemble an angel on a
snowflake, blooms in the bleak days of
winter, and gives assurance that the
earth is still alive.

Deep sleeps the Winter,
Cold, wet and grey;
Surely all the world is dead;
Spring is far away.
Wait! The world shall waken;
It is not dead, for lo,
The Fair Maids of February
Stand in the snow!

Moon Spirits

All white flowers have supernatural powers
because they are inhabited by moon spirits
that appear under a full moon. Do not bring
the Snowdrop indoors lest you should unleash
the spirits in your home.

As Pure as Snowdrops

The Snowdrop, with its pure white petals and
fresh green leaves, instills purity of thought to
the one who wears it.

Spindle Berry

◆ YOUR CHARMS ARE ENGRAVEN
ON MY HEART ◆

The Spindle tree carries this meaning because
its wood was used by sculptors for carving.
Later, as other woods replaced it for this
purpose, the Spindle Berry was primarily
used to make spindles – hence its name.

Strawberry

ESTEEM *&* LOVE ◆ PERFECT EXCELLENCE

Strawberry Blossom

◆ FORESIGHT ◆

In my party suit
Of red and white,
And a gift of fruit
For the feast tonight:

Strawberries small
And wild and sweet,
For the Queen and all
Of her court to eat!

The Strawberry's pretty white blossom
is tempting to pick, but those who
have foresight and resist its
charms will be rewarded
by its delicious fruit later.

Elfin Gifts

In Bavaria, the peasants tie a basket of
Strawberries between a cow's horns as a gift
for the elves, who are immensely fond of the
fruit. In return, the fairies ensure plentiful
supplies of milk to the peasants.

Sweet Chestnut

DO ME JUSTICE ◆ LUXURY

Like hedgehogs, their shells
Are prickly outside;
But silky within,
Where the little nuts hide,

Till the shell is split open,
And, shiny and fat,
The Chestnut appears;
Says the fairy: 'How's that?'

Concealed inside a prickly shell is a nut
that, once roasted, is deliciously sweet
and nutritious. Hence the Sweet
Chestnut, which looks unpleasant
at first, came to mean
'do me justice'.

Sweet Pea

◆ DELICATE PLEASURES ◆

Bride's Blessing

Sweet Peas should always be present at
weddings – they are good omens
for brides.

Tansy

◆ I DECLARE WAR AGAINST YOU ◆

In busy kitchens, in olden days,
Tansy was used in a score of ways;
Chopped and pounded,
when cooks would make
Tansy puddings and tansy cake,
Tansy posset, or tansy tea;
Physic or flavouring tansy'd be.

The Italians were not afraid to send Tansy –
and the message it conveyed – to
their enemies.

Tansy Skin Lotion

Soak a few leaves of Tansy in buttermilk for
nine days. Rub into skin to soften
and moisturise.

Tansy Tea

Tansy was grown in the kitchen garden for a
variety of dishes and remedies. Tansy tea was
brewed from fresh or dried tansy leaves and
calmed the nerves.

Totter-Grass

◆ AGITATION ◆

The leaves on the tree-tops
Dance in the breeze;
Totter-grass dances
And sways like the trees

Totter-grass is also called Quaking-grass
and means agitation because it
shivers in the breeze.

TRAVELLER'S JOY

◆ SAFETY TO TRAVELLERS ◆

Traveller, traveller, tramping by
To the seaport town where the big ships lie,
See, I have built a shady bower
To shelter you from the sun or shower.
Rest for a bit, then on, my boy!
Luck go with you, and Traveller's Joy!

Traveller's Joy is Wild Clematis; and when the
flowers are over, it becomes a mass of
silky fluff, which we call Old-Man's-Beard.

TULIP

BEAUTIFUL EYES ◆ FAME

Tulips originally came from Persia, and the
name Tulip comes from the Persian word for
turban, which the flower resembles. The
Tulip is a lucky charm for it ensures that its
owner will never go bareheaded for want
of a turban.

Bulbs in Butter

In the seventeenth century, Tulip bulbs were
considered a gourmet delicacy when boiled
and eaten with butter. During World War II,
when the Dutch were starving under German
occupation, Tulip bulbs shot up in price
because they had become a life-saving food.

Wallflower

FIDELITY IN ADVERSITY ◆ MISFORTUNE

Wallflower, Wallflower, up on the wall,
Who sowed your seed there?
'No one at all:
Long, long ago it was blown by the breeze
To the crannies of walls
where I live as I please.

Garden walls, castle walls, mossy and old,
These are my dwellings;
from these I behold
The changes of years…

The Wallflower originally grew wild in desolate places, climbing the walls of old ruins that had seen better days. Hence, it came to be associated with fidelity, because it stuck to its support for better or worse.

White Bindweed

INSINUATION ◆ HUMILITY

The Bindweed is the emblem of humility because it is too shy to show its flowers until it has gained the support of another plant on which it climbs.

White Clover

◆ THINK OF ME ◆

Lucky Clover

The rare four-leafed Clover is famous for bringing luck. Pick it with a gloved hand and give it to a mad person to cure them. It will also protect against being drafted into military service!

Make and Break a Fairy Spell

Lay seven grains of wheat upon a four leaved Clover and you will be able to see the fairies. Keep the Clover with you for it can break a fairy spell.

Clover Wedding

Lay a piece of Clover under your left garter to
ensure a large and fashionable wedding
in the Autumn.

WILD ROSE

PLEASURE & PAIN ◆ SIMPLICITY

The first Wild Rose found will strengthen
fraternal love.

WILLOW

FREEDOM ◆ MOURNING ◆ FORSAKEN

Wandering Willows

Willows are most active at night when they
uproot themselves and follow lone travellers,
whispering and muttering behind them.

To Mend a Broken Heart

Forsaken lovers carried a twig of Willow
because they believed that, being an emblem
of mourning, the Willow's heart would bear
the sorrow and save their own heart
from breaking.

The Toothache Spirit

In Japan, there is a superstition that the
Willow is inhabited by a spirit who will cure
toothache if the sufferer sticks pins
into the bark.

WINDFLOWER

SICKNESS ◆ EXPECTATION

The Windflower or Wood Anemone is the
emblem of expectation because it blooms
just before the return of the spring, and
is short-lived. For this reason it is
sometimes called April Fool.

Prairie Smoke

The Windflower is also called prairie smoke
because the smoke from the burning seed
pods was used to revive a person
from a faint.

YARROW

◆ WAR ◆

The Yarrow is also called Nosebleed because
it is effective in quelling the flow of blood.

Cot Guardian

Yarrow should be tied to the cradle of a
new-born infant to protect both child
and mother.

YEW

◆ SORROW ◆

I think of bygone centuries,
And seem to see anew
The archers face their enemies
With bended bows of Yew.

To Keep Witches Away

The Yew tree was sacred to the Druids, and is
associated with sorrow because it is almost
always planted in churchyards. For this
reason, it is disdained by witches who prefer
to avoid consecrated ground.

ZINNIA

◆ THOUGHTS OF ABSENT FRIENDS ◆

The reproductions in this book have been made using the most modern electronic scanning methods from entirely new transparencies of Cicely Mary Barker's original watercolours. They enable Cicely Mary Barker's skill as an artist to be appreciated as never before.

FREDERICK WARNE

Published by the Penguin Group
27 Wrights Lane, London W8 5TZ, England
Penguin Books USA Inc., 375 Hudson Street, New York, New York 10014, USA
Penguin Books Australia Ltd, Ringwood, Victoria, Australia
Penguin Books Canada Ltd, 10 Alcorn Avenue, Toronto, Ontario, Canada M4V 3B2
Penguin Books (NZ) Ltd, 182-190 Wairau Road, Auckland 10, New Zealand
Penguin Books Ltd, Registered Offices: Harmondsworth, Middlesex, England

First published in 1996

5 7 9 10 8 6 4

ISBN 0 7232 4291 7

Colour reproduction by Saxon
Printed and bound in Great Britain by William Clowes Limited,
Beccles and London